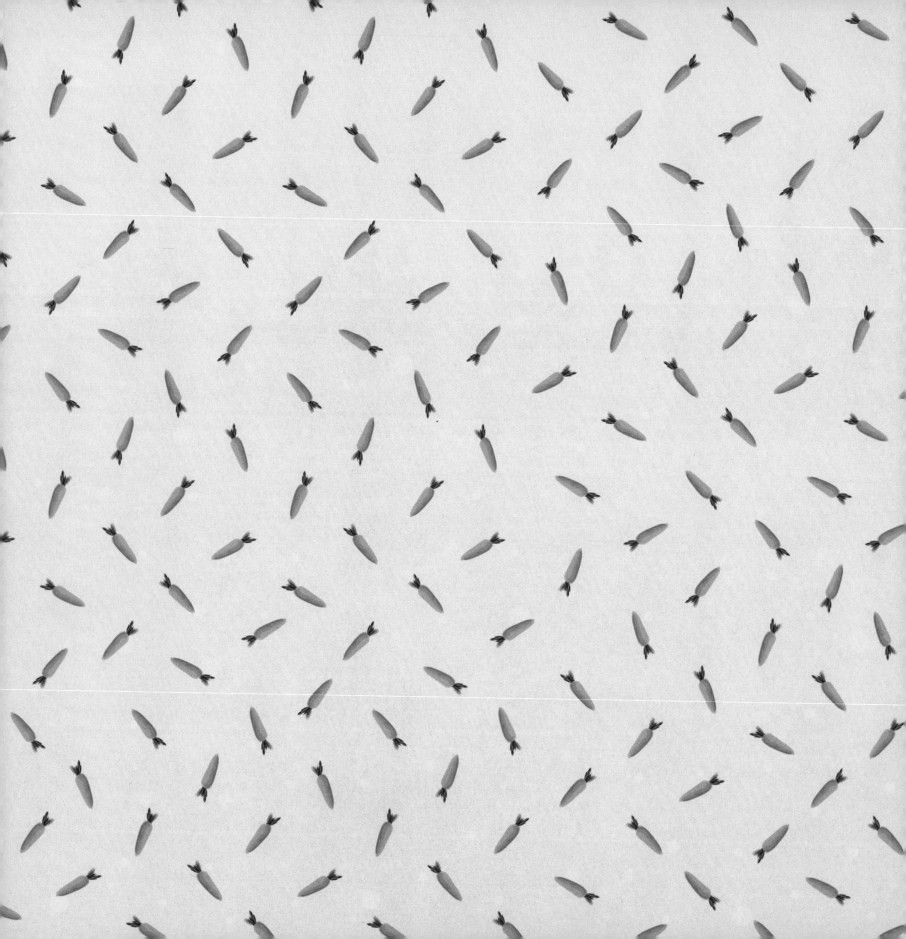

This book belongs to:

igloobooks

Published in 2018
by Igloo Books Ltd
Cottage Farm
Sywell
NN6 0BJ
www.igloobooks.com

Written by Stephanie Moss
Interiors illustrated by Adam Horsepool

Designed by Alex Alexandrou
Edited by Stephanie Moss

With special thanks to Psyop

STI002 1018
2 4 6 8 10 9 7 5 3 1
EAN 4088600100289

Printed and manufactured in the EU

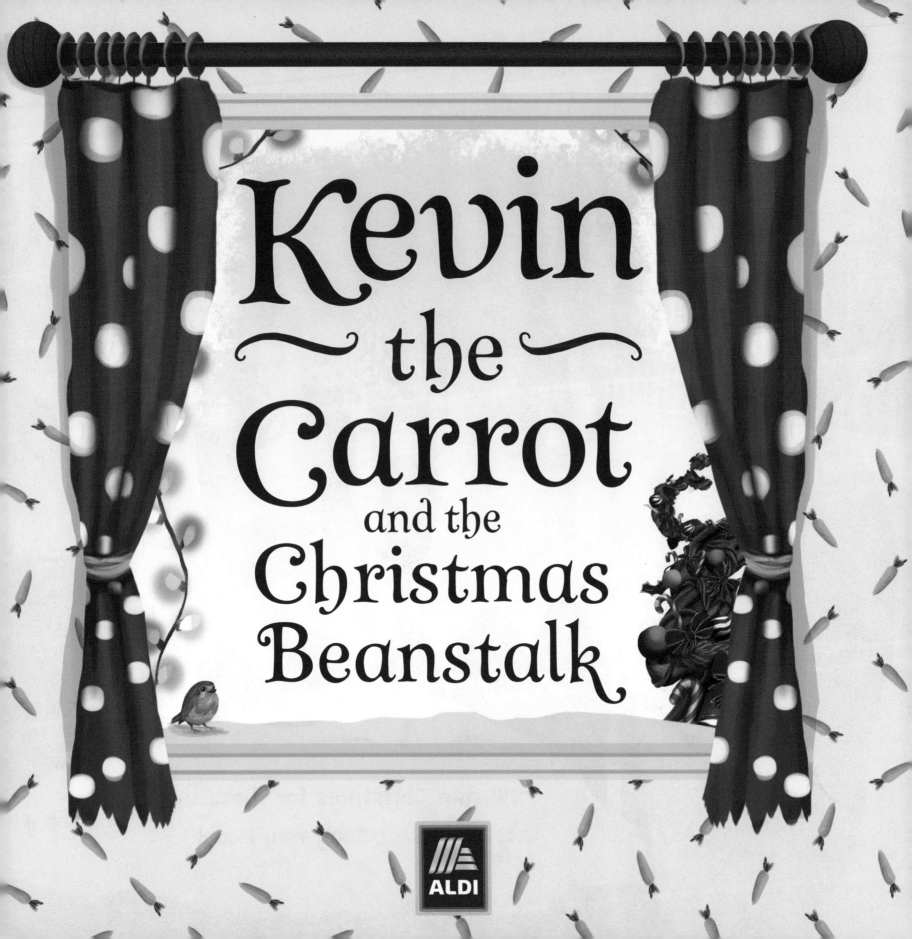

So he stole their decorations and their food for Christmas Day.

There were no presents for Jasper,
Baby or for Chantenay.

Kevin had an idea. Then, just like the fairy tale,
he set off on a journey to find magic beans for sale.

He threw them in the garden
when Katie had gone to bed.

Next he made a wish.
"Please save Christmas,"
Kevin said.

Then on Christmas Day,
Jasper cried, **"Guess what I can see!
It's a giant beanstalk
that looks like a Christmas tree!"**

"My wish came true,"
thought Kevin.
"I wonder what's up there?"

But Jasper was already
clambering into the air!

He dodged shiny baubles and red candy striped with white.
Then in a castle in the clouds he saw a most unpleasant sight.

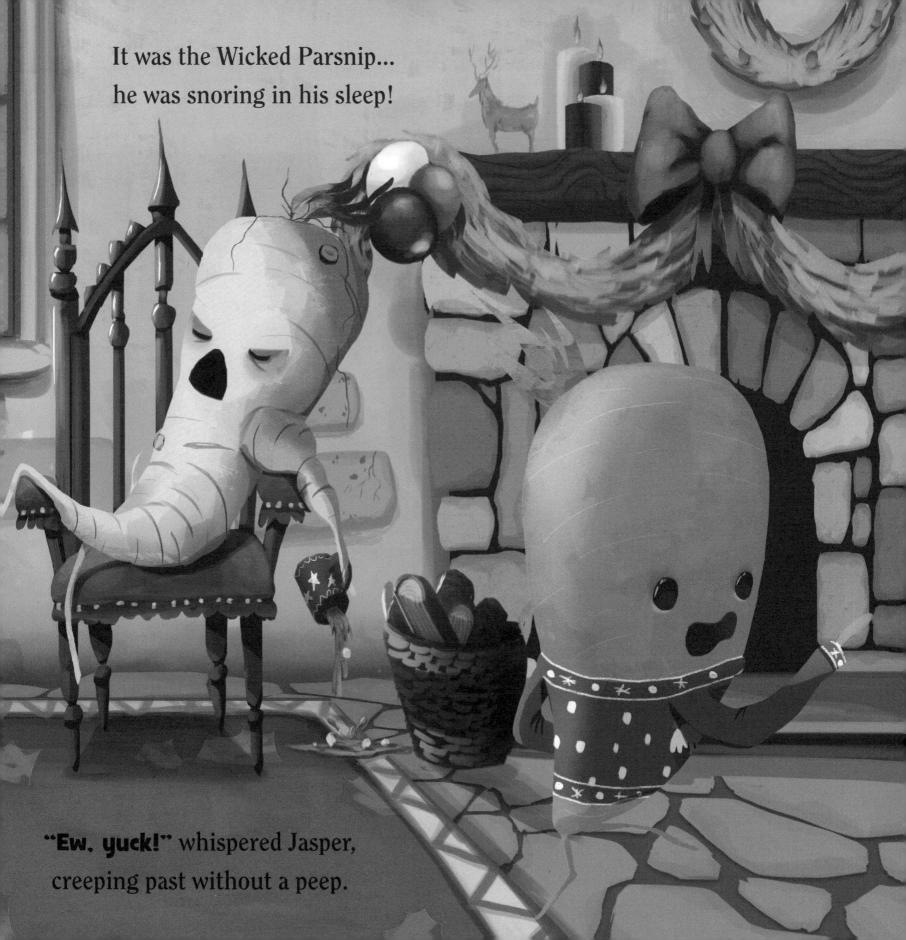

It was the Wicked Parsnip...
he was snoring in his sleep!

"Ew, yuck!" whispered Jasper,
creeping past without a peep.

Parsnip had their Christmas food. He'd put their gifts under his tree.
Jasper found their decorations and thought, **"I'll take those with me!"**

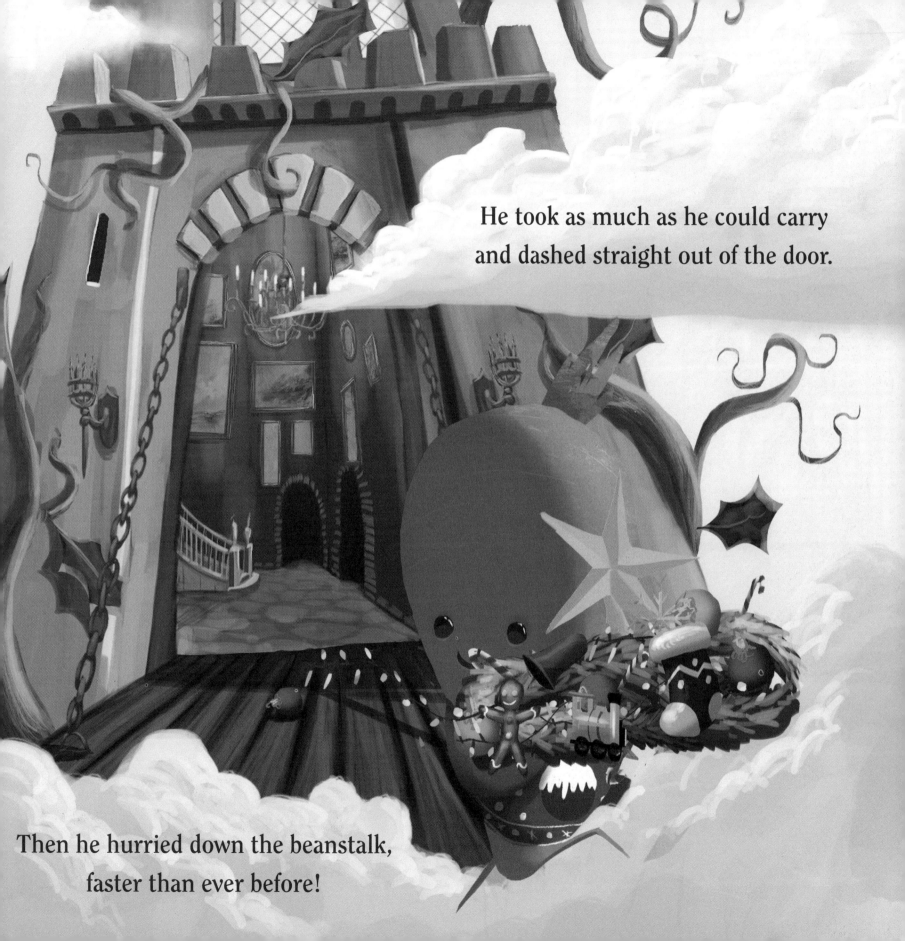

He took as much as he could carry
and dashed straight out of the door.

Then he hurried down the beanstalk,
faster than ever before!

Katie jumped up in the air
when Jasper brought everything back.
Baby thought he looked like Santa,
opening his Christmas sack.

"Me next!" cried Chantenay.
Then she scrambled out of sight.
**"I'll get our Christmas dinner back
before he takes one bite!"**

Chantenay found the Wicked Parsnip dancing to a little tune.
So she hid under the table, as he sang into a spoon.

Chantenay patiently waited, as he twirled and spun around.

Then she grabbed their Christmas dinner and raced back down to the ground.

Next Baby went to go and find their presents that were gone.
But the Wicked Parsnip saw him! Then the Christmas chase was on.

"Take that, Parsnip!" cried Baby, throwing presents in his way.
He got tangled in more tinsel than you'd find in Santa's sleigh.

At last Baby reached the beanstalk and he climbed down from the top.
Parsnip looked so red and angry, Baby thought that he might pop!

Baby slid down glittery tinsel
and whooshed past each
Christmas bow.
But the parsnip followed
closely till there wasn't
far to go.

With Baby safely on the ground, Kevin came to the rescue.
CHOP-CHOP went his shiny axe. CRASH went the beanstalk, too.

"Hip-hip-hooray!" cried Katie. **"Wicked Parsnip's gone forever!"**
And so the carrots spent the perfect Christmas Day together.